Geronimo Stilton
ENGLISH!

15 MONTHS AND SEASONS 月份和季節

新雅文化事業有限公司
www.sunya.com.hk

Geronimo Stilton English
MONTHS AND SEASONS 月份和季節

作　　者：Geronimo Stilton 謝利連摩・史提頓
譯　　者：申倩
責任編輯：王燕參
封面繪圖：Giuseppe Facciotto
插圖繪畫：Claudio Cernuschi, Andrea Denegri, Daria Cerchi
內文設計：Angela Ficarelli, Raffaella Picozzi
出　　版：新雅文化事業有限公司
　　　　　香港筲箕灣耀興道3號東匯廣場9樓
　　　　　營銷部電話：（852）2562 0161
　　　　　客戶服務部電話：（852）2976 6559
　　　　　傳真：（852）2597 4003
　　　　　網址：http://www.sunya.com.hk
　　　　　電郵：marketing@sunya.com.hk
發　　行：香港聯合書刊物流有限公司
　　　　　香港新界大埔汀麗路36號中華商務印刷大廈3字樓
　　　　　電話：（852）2150 2100　傳真：（852）2407 3062
　　　　　電郵：info@suplogistics.com.hk
印　　刷：C & C Offset Printing Co.,Ltd
　　　　　香港新界大埔汀麗路36號
版　　次：二〇一二年一月初版
　　　　　10 9 8 7 6 5 4 3 2 1

ISBN: 978-962-08-5489-7
© 2007 Edizioni Piemme S.p.A., Via Tiziano 32 - 20145 Milano - Italia
International Rights © 2007 Atlantyca S.p.A. - via Leopardi, 8, Milano - Italy
© 2012 for this Work in Traditional Chinese language, Sun Ya Publications (HK) Ltd.
9/F, Eastern Central Plaza, 3 Yiu Hing Rd, Shau Kei Wan, Hong Kong
Published and printed in Hong Kong

CONTENTS
目錄

BENJAMIN'S CLASSMATES
班哲文的老師和同學們

Maestra Topitilla
托比蒂拉·德·托比莉斯

Rarin
拉琳

Diego
迪哥

Rupa
露芭

Tui
杜爾

David
大衛

Sakura
櫻花

Mohamed
穆哈麥德

Tian Kai
田凱

Oliver
奧利佛

Milenko
米蘭哥

Trippo
特里普

Carmen
卡敏

Atina
阿提娜

Esmeralda
愛絲梅拉達

Pandora
潘朵拉

Takeshi
北野

Kuti
菊花

Benjamin
班哲文

Hsing
阿星

Laura
羅拉

Kiku
奇哥

Antonia
安東妮婭

Liza
麗莎

GERONIMO AND HIS FRIENDS
謝利連摩和他的家鼠朋友們

謝利連摩·史提頓 Geronimo Stilton
一個古怪的傢伙，簡直可以說是一隻笨拙的文化鼠。他是《鼠民公報》的總裁，正花盡心思改變報紙業的歷史。

菲·史提頓 Tea Stilton
謝利連摩的妹妹，她是《鼠民公報》的特派記者，同時也是一個運動愛好者。

班哲文·史提頓 Benjamin Stilton
謝利連摩的小姪兒，常被叔叔稱作「我的小乳酪」，是一隻感情豐富的小老鼠。

潘朵拉·華之鼠 Pandora Woz
柏蒂·活力鼠的姨甥女、班哲文最好的朋友，是一隻活潑開朗的小老鼠。

柏蒂·活力鼠 Patty Spring
美麗迷人的電視新聞工作者，致力於她熱愛的電視事業。

賴皮 Trappola
謝利連摩的表弟，非常喜歡食物，風趣幽默，是一隻饞嘴、愛開玩笑的老鼠，善於將歡樂傳遞給每一隻鼠。

麗萍姑媽 Zia Lippa
謝利連摩的姑媽，對鼠十分友善，又和藹可親，只想將最好的給身邊的鼠。

艾拿 Iena
謝利連摩的好朋友，充滿活力，熱愛各項運動，他希望能把對運動的熱誠傳給謝利連摩。

史奎克·愛管閒事鼠 Ficcanaso Squitt
謝利連摩的好朋友，是一個非常有頭腦的私家偵探，總是穿着一件黃色的乾濕褸。

SEASONS 季節

親愛的小朋友，你們貪吃嗎？我是很貪吃的，非常非常貪吃，而且越來越貪吃！我終於說服了瑪嘉蓮姑媽為我們焗製一個漂亮的蛋糕，她可是一個非常出色的廚師啊！我以一千塊莫澤雷勒乳酪發誓，那個蛋糕的香氣實在太誘人了！瑪嘉蓮姑媽說這是她的特製甜品——「四季蛋糕」！對了，你們想學習怎麼用英語說出四季的名稱嗎？我相信這一定難不倒你們的。

I'm going into the kitchen to make a "Four Seasons Cake"!

Perfect! A cake to say "spring, summer, autumn and winter" in English!

Good idea!

跟我謝利連摩．史提頓一起學英文，
就像玩遊戲一樣簡單好玩！

你可以一邊看着圖畫一邊讀。
以下有幾個標誌，你要特別留意：

🧀 當看到 💿 標誌時，你可以聽CD，
一邊聽，一邊跟着朗讀，還可以跟
着一起唱歌。

🧀 當看到 ✪ 標誌時，你可以和朋友
們一起玩遊戲，或者嘗試回答問
題。題目很簡單，它們對鞏固你所
學過的內容很有幫助。

🧀 當看到 ❗ 標誌時，你要注意看一
下格子裏的生字，反覆唸幾遍，掌
握發音。

最後，不要忘記完成小測驗和練習
冊裏的問題！看看你有多聰明吧。

祝大家學得開開心心！

謝利連摩．史提頓

SPRING 春天

漫長的冬天過去後，便是春天。在春天裏，大自然的一切都蘇醒過來。和暖的太陽照耀着大地，草地上開滿了美麗的鮮花。

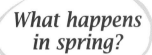

What happens in spring?

In spring

new leaves grow on the branches of trees.

In spring

strawberries ripen.

In spring

swallows prepare their nests.

Children, what do you do in spring?

In spring we play outdoors, in the school yard during our break.

In spring I look at the flowers that are starting to grow in the garden.

In spring I pick strawberries with Grandma Rosa.

In spring I play in the park after school.

In spring I wear my short-sleeved T-shirts.

look at
看着

pick
摘

 試着用英語説出：「在春天，放學後我會到公園玩耍。」

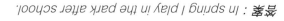

SUMMER 夏天

夏天的天氣真熱啊！還好在太陽最猛烈的時候，我們可以吃一片冰涼的西瓜，或者吃一個加了乳酪的雪糕球消消暑，真是涼透心！

What happens in summer?

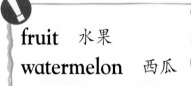

fruit　水果
watermelon　西瓜

In summer swallows bring food to their little ones who are learning to fly.

In summer trees are full of fruit.

In summer people eat watermelon.

Children, what do you do in summer?

In summer schools are closed. We are on holiday!

In summer I read many exciting books!

In summer I go on holiday to the seaside.

We read comics!

⭐ 試着用英語説出：
「夏天放假時，我會到海邊去。」

In summer I often go on bicycle rides with Aunt Patty.

In summer I go on holiday to the mountains!

答案：In summer I go on holiday to the seaside.

AUTUMN 秋天

秋天有不同顏色的樹葉，多美啊！我最喜歡在秋天去郊遊，你呢？

What happens in autumn?

In autumn swallows migrate.

In autumn there are grapes and chestnuts.
秋天有葡萄和栗子。

In autumn trees lose their leaves.

In autumn there are grapes and chestnuts.

Children, what do you do in autumn?

The Seasons

Butterflies and flowers
in springtime you will find
but when the sun is in the sky
and the hot weather comes
summer's here, we go to the beach.
Autumn, winter, spring and summer,
the four seasons, happy and funny,
they are beautiful and coloured
every year they return.
Chestnuts, grapes and mushrooms
in autumn you will find
but when the snow slowly falls
I play with my friends.
Winter's here,
it'll be Christmas soon.
Autumn, winter, spring and summer,
the four seasons, happy and funny,
they are beautiful and coloured
every year they return.

In autumn

we go back to school, we meet our teachers and friends again.

In autumn

I go to pick chestnuts with Aunt Patty.

⭐ 試着用英語說出:「在秋天, 我回到學校上課。」

WINTER 冬天

冬天的天氣很冷，外出時，記得要穿上厚厚的大衣啊！

What happens in winter?

Children, what do you do in winter?

In winter the birds that don't migrate look for crumbs and seeds on perches.

In winter many trees lose all their leaves.

In winter I drink a cup of hot chocolate to get warm.

14

It's cold in winter! I put on my anorak and my boots.

In winter we go ice-skating.

I go skiing.
我去滑雪。
We go ice-skating.
我們去溜冰。

In winter I go skiing in the mountains.

I make a snowman!

In winter

we all sing together around a Christmas tree.

⭐ 試着用英語說出：「在冬天，我到山上去滑雪。」

THE MONTHS OF THE YEAR 月份

一年有四季，就像瑪嘉蓮姑媽做的蛋糕的名字一樣。而一年有十二個月，就像賴皮吃掉一份蛋糕所花的時間一樣——十二秒！現在我們一起來學習怎樣用英語說出十二個月份的名稱吧！

January 一月

It's the first month of the year. It brings snow!

February 二月

It's the second month of the year. We put masks on and throw confetti into the air.

March 三月

It's the third month of the year. Flowers blossom in the meadows and on the trees.

April 四月

It's the fourth month of the year. On the first day of this month we play tricks on our friends.

May 五月

It's the fifth month of the year. Roses bloom in gardens.

June 六月

It's the sixth month of the year. Lots of people go to the seaside and dive into the waves.

July 七月

It's the seventh month of the year. Schools close and we go on holiday.

August 八月

It's the eighth month of the year. Some people go walking in the mountains.

September 九月

It's the ninth month of the year. School starts again and we meet our teachers and friends.

October 十月

It's the tenth month of the year. We go picking chestnuts.

November 十一月

It's the eleventh month of the year. We stay at home where it's nice and warm.

December 十二月

It's the twelfth month of the year. We decorate the Christmas tree.

❗ lots of people 很多人

❗

1st. the first
第一

2nd. the second
第二

3rd. the third
第三

4th. the fourth
第四

5th. the fifth
第五

6th. the sixth
第六

7th. the seventh
第七

8th. the eighth
第八

9th. the ninth
第九

10th. the tenth
第十

11th. the eleventh
第十一

12th. the twelfth
第十二

I WAS BORN IN...
我是……月出生的

瑪嘉蓮姑媽的特色蛋糕終於做好了，我急不及待要嘗一嘗，但瑪嘉蓮姑媽說要等它先冷卻才可以吃。在等待的時候，我請班哲文和他的朋友們說說他們是幾月出生的。

I was born in January!

I was born in February!

I was born in March!

I was born in April!

I was born in May!

I was born in June!

I was born in July!

I was born in August!

I was born in September!

I was born in October!

I was born in November!

I was born in December!

⭐ 你是幾月出生的？試着用英語說出來。**I was born in ....**

MY BIRTHDAY IS ON...
我的生日是……

接着，我還教大家用英語說出自己的
生日日期呢！

My birthday is on the second of June.

Kiku's birthday is on the 2nd of June.

My birthday is on the eighteenth of January.

Esmeralda's birthday is on the 18th of January.

A SONG FOR YOU! Track 2

Twelve Little Friends

January, February,
March, April, May,
June, July,
August, September,
October, November, December...
these are twelve little friends
over and over and over again!

⭐ 你是幾月幾日出生的？試着用英語說出來。

My birthday is on the … of … .

13th • the thirteenth 第十三	23rd • the twenty-third 第二十三
14th • the fourteenth 第十四	24th • the twenty-fourth 第二十四
15th • the fifteenth 第十五	25th • the twenty-fifth 第二十五
16th • the sixteenth 第十六	26th • the twenty-sixth 第二十六
17th • the seventeenth 第十七	27th • the twenty-seventh 第二十七
18th • the eighteenth 第十八	28th • the twenty-eighth 第二十八
19th • the nineteenth 第十九	29th • the twenty-ninth 第二十九
20th • the twentieth 第二十	30th • the thirtieth 第三十
21st • the twenty-first 第二十一	31st • the thirty-first 第三十一
22nd • the twenty-second 第二十二	

〈登上世界最高峯〉

艾拿和謝利連摩正在爬上世界最高峯⋯⋯
艾拿：謝利連摩，你有沒有感到很自豪呀？
謝利連摩：噢，有啊！爬山真是一種很美妙的經歷啊！

謝利連摩：現在我能真正體會到爬山的意義了。

艾拿：嗯，但要小心你手爪放的位置。

艾拿：說到底，你還是畏高的。　　　　謝利連摩：但我今天沒事。我只需吃一些朱古力和……

謝利連摩：……喝一口這些泉水。

艾拿：謝利連摩，小心啊！

謝利連摩：我忘記在這麼冷的天氣下，水都結成冰了。

艾拿：你說得對！

謝利連摩：幸好這裏有大量冰塊，可以用來敷我撞傷的部位。

艾拿：有聲音！會不會是傳說中的雪怪呢？
謝利連摩：我們走過去看看吧。

謝利連摩：他在那裏，就像我所想的一樣……

謝利連摩：雪怪正在冬眠。他忘記了關掉電視機！我們把它關上吧！
艾拿：我們現在走吧……

謝利連摩：現在我們不要再浪費時間了！我們只需再努力一點就……

謝利連摩：妙鼠城的旗子終於插在世界最高峯上，隨風飄揚了！

艾拿：謝謝你，謝利連摩！真是妙極了！

班哲文：叔叔，是時候要走了！
謝利連摩：我正想爬下來。

The End

艾拿：那麼，我們什麼時候去爬山的另一面呢？
謝利連摩：明天……但只是限於拍電影！

TEST 小測驗

⭐ 1. 用英語說出四季的名稱。

(a)  (b) 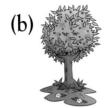 (c)  (d)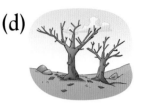

⭐ 2. 用英語說出下面的詞彙：

(a) 士多啤梨	**(b)** 栗子	**(c)** 西瓜	**(d)** 葉子
(e) 樹	**(f)** 葡萄	**(g)** 燕子	**(h)** 花

⭐ 3. 讀出下面的句子，並用中文說出句子的意思。

(a) *I go on holiday to the seaside in summer.*

(b) *I go on holiday to the mountains in summer!*

⭐ 4. 下圖中的小朋友正在做什麼？試着用英語說出來。

(a)

We go ... .

(b)

I go ... in the mountains.

⭐ 5. 你會用英語說出十二個月份的名稱嗎？說說看。

⭐ 6. 四月和六月之間是哪一個月？用英語回答。

April   ...   June

Track 4

DICTIONARY 詞典

（英、粵、普發聲）

A

a cup of　一杯

afraid of　害怕

anorak　禦寒外套

April　四月

August　八月

autumn　秋天

B

beach　海灘

beautiful　美麗

bicycle rides　騎單車
　（普：騎自行車）

birds　小鳥

birthday　生日

blossom　盛開

boots　靴子

born　出生

branches　樹枝

butterflies　蝴蝶

C

cake　蛋糕

chestnuts　栗子

chocolate　朱古力
　（普：巧克力）

Christmas tree　聖誕樹

climbing　爬

cold　冷

comics　漫畫

D

December　十二月

decorate　裝飾

dive　跳水

drink　喝

E

effort　努力

experience　經歷

F

February　二月

film　電影

flag　旗子

flowers　花

fly　飛

food　食物

forgot　忘記

freezes　結冰

friends　朋友

fruit　水果

funny　有趣

G

garden　花園

go away　走開

good idea　好主意

grapes　葡萄

grow　生長

H

happens　發生

hibernation　冬眠

hot　熱

I

ice　冰

ice-skating　溜冰

J

January　一月

July　七月

June　六月

K

kitchen　廚房

L

leaves　葉子

look at　看着

look for 尋找

lose 失去

M

make 製造

March 三月

masks 面具

May 五月

meadows 草地

month 月份

mountains 山

mushrooms 蘑菇

N

nests 鳥巢

noise 噪音

November 十一月

O

October 十月

outdoors 戶外

P

park 公園

people 人們

play 玩耍

play tricks on 作弄

prepare 預備

put 放

put on 穿上

R

ripen 成熟

roses 玫瑰

S

school 學校

sea 海

seaside 海邊

seasons 季節

seeds 種子

September 九月

short-sleeved 短袖

sing 唱歌

skiing　滑雪

snow　雪

snowman　雪人

spring　春天

strawberries　士多啤梨
　　（普：草莓）

summer　夏天

sun　太陽

swallows　燕子

switch off　關掉

wasting　浪費

watch out　小心

watermelon　西瓜

wear　穿

weather　天氣

winter　冬天

Y

yard　院子

T

teachers　老師

thanks to　多謝

throw　拋

time　時間

trees　樹

walking　走路

W

warm　溫暖

看在一千塊莫澤雷勒乳酪的份上，你學得開心嗎？很開心，對不對？好極了！跟你一起跳舞唱歌我也很開心！我等着你下次繼續跟班哲文和潘朵拉一起玩一起學英語呀。現在要說再見了，當然是用英語說啦！

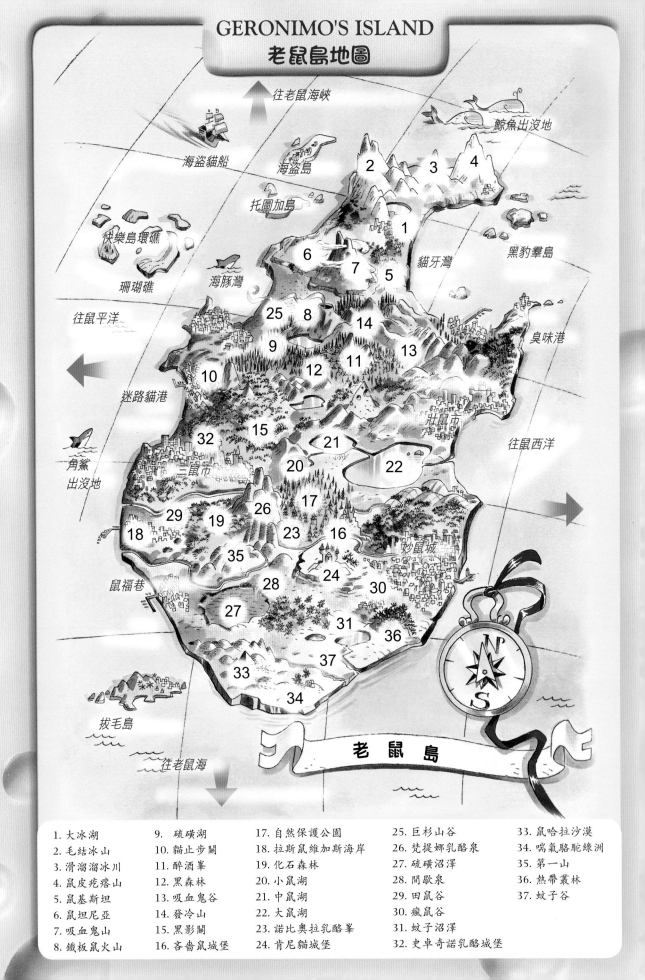

GERONIMO'S ISLAND
老鼠島地圖

往老鼠海峽

鯨魚出沒地

海盜貓船

海盜島

托圖加島

黑豹羣島

快樂島環礁

珊瑚礁　海豚灣

往鼠平洋

迷路貓港

臭味港

往鼠西洋

角鯊
出沒地

三鼠市

壯鼠市

妙鼠城

鼠福巷

拔毛島

往老鼠海

老鼠島

1. 大冰湖	9. 硫磺湖	17. 自然保護公園	25. 巨杉山谷	33. 鼠哈拉沙漠
2. 毛結冰山	10. 貓止步關	18. 拉斯鼠維加斯海岸	26. 梵提娜乳酪泉	34. 喘氣駱駝綠洲
3. 滑溜溜冰川	11. 醉酒峯	19. 化石森林	27. 硫磺沼澤	35. 第一山
4. 鼠皮疙瘩山	12. 黑森林	20. 小鼠湖	28. 間歇泉	36. 熱帶叢林
5. 鼠基斯坦	13. 吸血鬼谷	21. 中鼠湖	29. 田鼠谷	37. 蚊子谷
6. 鼠坦尼亞	14. 發冷山	22. 大鼠湖	30. 瘋鼠谷	
7. 吸血鬼山	15. 黑影關	23. 諾比奧拉乳酪峯	31. 蚊子沼澤	
8. 鐵板鼠火山	16. 客嗇鼠城堡	24. 肯尼貓城堡	32. 史卓奇諾乳酪城堡	

Geronimo Stilton

EXERCISE BOOK
練習冊

想知道自己對 MONTHS AND SEASONS 掌握了多少，
趕快打開後面的練習完成它吧！

ENGLISH!

15 **MONTHS AND SEASONS** 月份和季節

SEASONS 季節

⭐ 1. 你知道下面的圖畫各代表什麼季節嗎？在橫線上填上正確的
　　字母找出答案吧。

(a)

__ u t __ m __

(b)
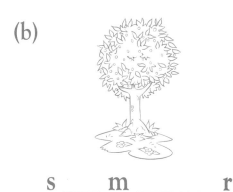

s __ m __ __ r

(c)

__ __ n t __ r

(d)
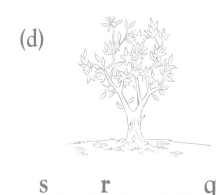

s __ r __ __ g

⭐ 2. 看看下面的問題，選出正確的答案填在橫線上。

spring	summer	autumn	winter

(a) The season before winter is _____ .

(b) The season after winter is _____ .

(c) The season between autumn and spring is _____ .

WHAT ARE THEY DOING?
他們在做什麼？

⭐ 下圖中的小朋友在做什麼？把代表答案的英文字母填在 ☐ 內。

A. I play in the park in spring.

B. I go back to school in autumn.

C. I go on holiday to the mountains in summer.

D. I go skiing in winter.

1. ☐

2. ☐

3. ☐

4. ☐

WHAT ARE THEY SAYING?
他們在說什麼？

⭐ 下圖中的小朋友在說什麼？把圖畫和相應的句框用線連起來。

1.

A.

Schools are closed, I am on holiday!

2.

B.

I make a snowman!

3.

C.

I go back to school, I meet my teachers and friends.

FIND THE RIGHT WORDS
選詞填空

⭐ 根據圖畫，選出適當的字詞填在橫線上，完成句子。

chestnuts   strawberries
ice-skating   comics

1. We read _____ !

2. I pick _____ with Grandma Rosa.

3. I go to pick _____ with Aunt Patty.

4. We go_____ .

THE MONTHS OF THE YEAR 月份

⭐ 你知道下面各個月份的英文名稱嗎？把字母重新排列好，並在橫線上寫出來。

1. 一月 UNJRYAA
   _____

2. 二月 BREFARUY
   _____

3. 三月 CHMAR
   _____

4. 四月 LIRPA
   _____

5. 五月 YMA
   _____

6. 六月 UENJ
   _____

7. 七月 LYJU
   _____

8. 八月 UUGTSA
   _____

9. 九月 PETMEREBS
   _____

10. 十月 BEROOTC
    _____

11. 十一月 MBREVENO
    _____

12. 十二月 MEBERDCE
    _____

5

DO YOU KNOW?
你知道嗎？

⭐ 你知道下面的句子所描述的是哪一個月份嗎？在橫線上填寫正確的答案。

1.
It's the sixth month of the year.
It's _____ .

2.
It's the eighth month of the year.
It's _____ .

3.
It's the third month of the year.
It's _____ .

4.
It's the twelfth month of the year.
It's _____ .

5.
It's the tenth month of the year.
It's _____ .

6.
It's the eleventh month of the year.
It's _____ .

7.
It's the ninth month of the year.
It's _____ .

8.
It's the fifth month of the year.
It's _____ .

MY BIRTHDAY IS ON...
我的生日是⋯⋯⋯

⭐ 1. 你是幾月出生的？你的生日是幾月幾日？試着在橫線上填寫答案，然後讀出句子。

(a) I was born in _____ .

(b) My birthday is on the _____ of _____ .

⭐ 2. 依指示完成下列各題。（答案可圈多於一個）

(a) Which months have thirty days?
Circle them with a red crayon.

(b) Which months have thirty-one days?
Circle them with a green crayon.

(c) Which months has twenty-eight days clear, and twenty-nine days in each leap year? Circle them with a blue crayon.

January	February	March
April	May	June
July	August	September
October	November	December

ANSWERS 答案

TEST 小測驗

1. (a) spring   (b) summer   (c) autumn   (d) winter
2. (a) strawberry / strawberries   (b) chestnut / chestnuts   (c) watermelon   (d) leaf / leaves
      (e) tree / trees   (f) grape / grapes   (g) swallow / swallows   (h) flower / flowers
3. (a) 夏天放假時，我會到海邊去。   (b) 夏天放假時，我會到山上去。
4. (a) We go ice-skating.   (b) I go skiing in the mountains.
5. January, February, March, April, May, June, July, August, September, October, November, December
6. May

EXERCISE BOOK 練習冊

P.1

1. (a) a u t u m n   (b) s u m m e r   (c) w i n t e r   (d) s p r i n g
2. (a) autumn   (b) spring   (c) summer / winter

P.2

1. A   2. C   3. B   4. D

P.3

1. B   2. A   3. C

P.4

1. comics   2. strawberries   3. chestnuts   4. ice-skating

P.5

1. JANUARY   2. FEBRUARY   3. MARCH   4. APRIL   5. MAY   6. JUNE   7. JULY
8. AUGUST   9. SEPTEMBER   10. OCTOBER   11. NOVEMBER   12. DECEMBER

P.6

1. June   2. August   3. March   4. December   5. October   6. November   7. September   8. May

P.7

1. 根據實際情況作答。
2. (a) April, June, September, November
   (b) January, March, May, July, August, October, December
   (c) February